The Rugrats and the Zombies

by Sarah Willson

illustrated by Barry Goldberg

SIMON SPOTLIGHT/NICKELODEON

Based on the TV series *Rugrats*® created by Klasky/Csupo Inc.
and Paul Germain as seen on Nickelodeon®

SIMON SPOTLIGHT
An imprint of Simon & Schuster Children's Publishing Division
1230 Avenue of the Americas
New York, New York 10020

Manufactured in the United States of America
First Edition   10 9 8 7 6 5 4 3 2
ISBN 0-689-82125-5

"Drats!" fumed Angelica, as she stomped around the Pickleses' living room.

"What's the matter?" asked Tommy.

She whirled around. "I'll tell you what. While my mom and dad are outta town this week, I'm stuck here with you babies. And every day—for three hours!—they're showing back-to-back Shirlylock Holmes episodes on TV. Today they're showing my favorite episode, 'Shirlylock and the Zombies'!"

"What's wrong with that?" asked Chuckie.

"I'm only allowed to watch a *half hour* of TV a day!"

Tommy's mother Didi came into the room.

"Here are some activities for you, Angelica," Didi said cheerfully. "These will help develop your math skills! This one's called 'Kiddie Kalculus'! You can work on it while the babies take their naps!" She left for the kitchen.

"Well, at least you babies will be outta my hair for a while," scowled Angelica. "Now, how can I get the grown-ups to disappear too, so I can watch TV in peace?" she muttered to herself.

Suddenly a sly look crossed her face.

"Uh, did I mention that we . . . er . . . have an emergency on our hands?" Angelica said. She held up the cover of the TV listings. "It says here that when parents get up late they turn into . . . zombies!"

"Wh-wh-what are zombies?" asked Chuckie.

"They look like this," she said, pointing to the picture. "Zombies fly into houses searching for parents who are sleeping late. They take over their bodies and turn their brains into mush—so they become zombies too! And everybody knows zombies like nothing more than to terrify babies!"

"Aaaaaaah!" cried the babies.

So the next morning, the babies woke their parents early.

At the grocery store, Didi put groceries in the baby car seat and loaded Tommy into the back of the car.

"Waaaah!" cried Tommy.

"Oh, dear. Sorry, honey," said Didi absently. "I don't know what's happening to my brain today!"

Back home, Tommy's father put the ice cream into the cupboard.

"Guess I'll go down to the basement to work now, Deed," said Stu.

Tommy watched his father walk into a closet. "They're turning into zombies!" he wailed softly to himself.

The next morning the babies woke their parents even earlier.
"You sure are getting up early these days, Champ,"
mumbled Stu. He put a bowl of dog food in front of Tommy.
Then he put a baby bottle in front of Tommy's dog, Spike.
"What are we going to do, Stu?" asked Didi blearily, as she
stirred mustard into her coffee.
"Do, Stu . . . Stu do . . . Sue too . . ." was all Stu could mumble.
"Waaaaaaah!" wailed Tommy.

"It's not working!" whimpered Chuckie later that day. "My dad is turning into a zombie! He dressed me in my winter coat this morning—and it's warm out!"

"Yeah, our parents are zombies too!" said Phil.

"Our mom dressed us in bathing suits today!" said Lil.

"My mom wore her slippers to the grocery store," said Tommy miserably.

"They're turning into zombies all right," said Angelica, who was listening gleefully.

That afternoon everyone in Tommy's house took a long nap. Everyone except Angelica.

"It's working! They're all outta the way for the whole afternoon!" she cackled to herself as she settled in to watch Shirlylock Holmes.

The next morning Tommy woke his parents even earlier.

"Deed, what are we going to do?" asked Stu, buttering the newspaper.

"Let's take the kids to see Dr. Lipschitz. He'll know what to do," said Didi.

"You call Betty and Howard and Chaz. I'll go get my bathrobe," responded Stu.

Later that day the parents took the babies to the Lipschitz sleep-disorder clinic. They left Angelica with Grandpa, who immediately fell asleep.

"Shirlylock, here I come!" said Angelica, zapping on the TV.

At the clinic Dr. Lipschitz listened gravely to what the grown-ups had to say. "Eliminate their afternoon naps," he declared, and handed them their bill.

Because they hadn't napped the day before, the tired babies slept in the next morning. So did their parents.

"You know, I think Angelica was playing a trick on us," yawned Tommy to his friends. "My mom and dad woke up late this morning, and they've stopped acting like zombies."

"Same with my dad," said Chuckie. Phil and Lil nodded.

"You know what I think?" Tommy continued. "I think Angelica wanted the growed-ups to be so tired, they'd take naps, so she could watch TV."

That afternoon Angelica ran into the living room and grabbed the clicker.
"Outta my way, you babies!" she yelled.
"It's Shirlylock time!"

Didi and Stu walked in just as Angelica was turning on the TV.

"Uh-uh-uh, Angelica, dear," said Didi, when she noticed the TV was on.

"Okay, Aunt Didi," said Angelica sweetly. "But isn't it time for all of you to take your naps?"

"No more naps!" said Stu.

"Huh?" said Angelica.

"Here you are, Angelica," said Didi. "Your mom left these instructional playthings for you to amuse yourself with."

"You know what?" Tommy whispered to his friends.
"I think Angelica might be the one turning into a zombie."